Toothpaste

BEFORE THE STORE

BY JAN BERNARD • ILLUSTRATED BY DAN McGEEHAN

Published by The Child's World®
1980 Lookout Drive • Mankato, MN 56003-1705
800-599-READ • www.childsworld.com

ACKNOWLEDGMENTS
The Child's World®: Mary Berendes, Publishing Director
The Design Lab: Design and production
Red Line Editorial: Editorial direction
Content Consultant: S. Jack Hu, Ph.D., J. Reid and Polly Anderson Professor of Manufacturing
Technology, Professor of Mechanical Engineering and Industrial and Operations Engineering,
The University of Michigan

ISBN 9781609736842
LCCN 2011940080

PHOTO CREDITS
Maria Gritcai/Dreamstime, cover, 1, back cover; Antiode/Dreamstime, cover (inset), 1 (inset); Debbi
Smirnoff/iStockphoto, 5; Tolga Tezcan/iStockphoto, 7; Jaimie Duplass/Bigstock, 9; Shawn Hempel/
Shutterstock Images, 10; Cheryl Davis/iStockphoto, 11; Natallia Yaumenenka/iStockphoto, 15; Sabina
Schaaf/iStockphoto, 21; Alexandru Kacso/iStockphoto, 23; Marek Kosmal/iStockphoto, 29

Design elements: Maria Gritcai/Dreamstime

Printed in the United States of America

ABOUT THE AUTHOR

Jan Bernard has been an elementary teacher in both Ohio and in Georgia and has written curriculum for schools for more than seven years. She lives in West Jefferson, Ohio, with her husband Tom and their dog, Nigel. She has two sons who live in Columbus, Ohio.

Contents

CHAPTER ONE

A Tooth Scrubber!

Did you know that your teeth are cleaned with rocks? That may sound strange, but it is true! Some of these tiny rocks are called **abrasives**. These pieces of rock are much smaller than grains of sand! They are part of what makes toothpaste such a great tooth scrubber. Abrasives scratch and grind at the surface of something. They remove tiny pieces of food stuck in your teeth. They also take away **plaque** on the surface of teeth. Toothpaste has many other **ingredients**, too. Lots of these are made from minerals that come from rocks. Some ingredients make

We use toothpaste to scrub our teeth clean.

your teeth whiter. Some keep your breath smelling fresh. Together, they keep your teeth healthy and clean.

Have you thought about how toothpaste is made? First the toothpaste factory buys **chemicals** used in the toothpaste. These chemicals are made in labs at chemical companies. Then they are shipped to toothpaste factories in large bags or containers. Now it is time to make the toothpaste! There are many steps. The first step starts with the toothpaste recipe. Every toothpaste company has its own special recipe. But some things are common in all brands of toothpaste.

Toothpaste is made from rock minerals.

CHAPTER TWO

The Toothpaste Recipe

Abrasives are the power scrubbers in toothpaste. Binders are also needed. They make toothpaste smooth and thick. Binders keep the ingredients mixed together in a paste. That is important because it helps toothpaste stay on your toothbrush!

Sudsers are foaming bubbles. They help get rid of food pieces. They also help keep toothpaste from dribbling out of your mouth and down your chin! Toothpaste needs a **humectant**. It keeps water in the

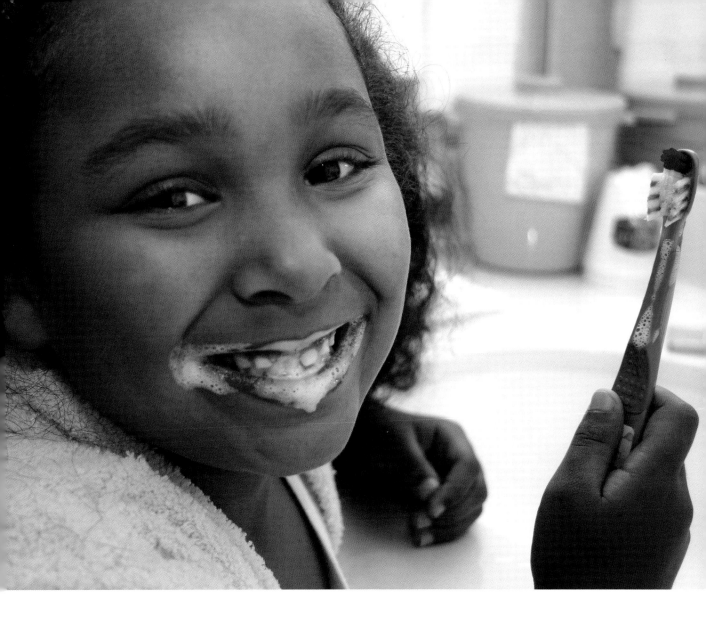

toothpaste. The toothpaste stays moist, so it feels good in your mouth.

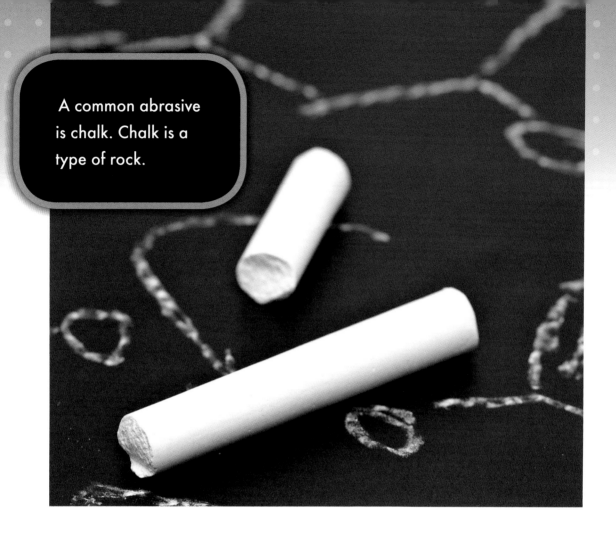

A common abrasive is chalk. Chalk is a type of rock.

Toothpaste needs to taste good so you will keep using it. Flavor oils add the fresh taste people like. The oils also help keep your breath smelling good. Some toothpaste companies use natural flavor oils. These oils are made from herbs such as peppermint. Most

Chalk is an example of a rock that can grind away food particles.

Eat your vegetables! They can help clean your teeth. Cucumbers, carrots, and celery are natural abrasives.

large toothpaste companies use chemicals to make the oil. All flavor oils have both taste and smell. Fluoride is added to make your teeth strong. Whiteners are added to make your teeth look whiter. Whiteners work by getting rid of stains on tooth **enamel**.

Vegetables are common natural abrasives that can help keep your teeth clean.

CHAPTER THREE

A Toothpaste Factory

The different ingredients are weighed and tested for quality. It is important that each ingredient is just right! First water is mixed with the humectant in a large container called a mixing vat. The water and humectant mix then goes through pipes to another part of the factory. That part of the factory is called the make area. That is where the rest of the ingredients are added.

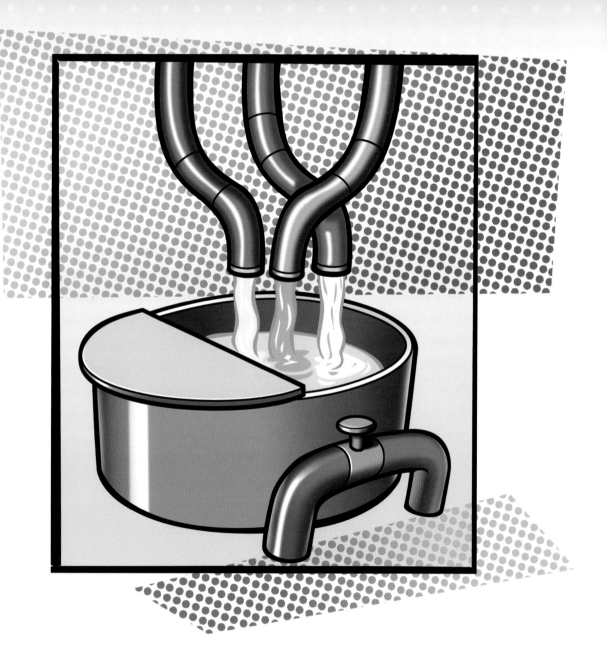

Ingredients are mixed in a mixing vat.

The ingredients are mixed together in a large vat. This vat is like a very large pot. Its lid has mixing blades. Some vats hold enough toothpaste to make 10,000 tubes. Bigger vats hold enough toothpaste to make 30,000 tubes!

Workers add abrasives to the mix. If the abrasive is chalk, it goes into a giant sifter. This sifts out the big pieces, so only tiny pieces go into the toothpaste. Then workers add sudsers and flavor oils to the mix. Some popular flavors are peppermint and cinnamon.

Most toothpaste has fluoride, which is added next. If the toothpaste is going to be a whitening

type, then a whitener is also used. **Preservatives** are added so the toothpaste can stay on a store's shelf for a long time. Sweeteners are added to make the toothpaste taste good.

Finally the ingredients are heated together inside the vat. The mixing blades move through the mixture. The toothpaste becomes smooth and shiny.

Cinnamon and mint are two popular toothpaste flavors.

CHAPTER FOUR

Cooling the Toothpaste

After the toothpaste has been mixed and heated, it has to be cooled. The toothpaste now looks like gooey dough. Workers raise the lid of the vat and scrape and clean the large mixing blades. None of the toothpaste is wasted. It is kind of like cleaning frosting off a really big mixer! Next workers test small samples of the toothpaste batch. The testers make sure each batch tastes good and is smooth. A machine also tests the toothpaste to make sure it has the right amount of water. A worker throws away batches that do not pass the tests.

Workers scrape the toothpaste off the mixing blades.

CHAPTER FIVE

Filling the Tubes

Good batches of toothpaste can move on in the factory. The batches go through hoses to filling machines. These machines fill the toothpaste tubes.

First workers put toothpaste tubes on a **conveyor belt**. The caps are already on, but the bottom is open. The tubes go to the filling machine with the cap side down. A machine blows air into the tubes to remove dust. A machine holds the tube in place. Then a filling machine squirts just enough toothpaste into each tube.

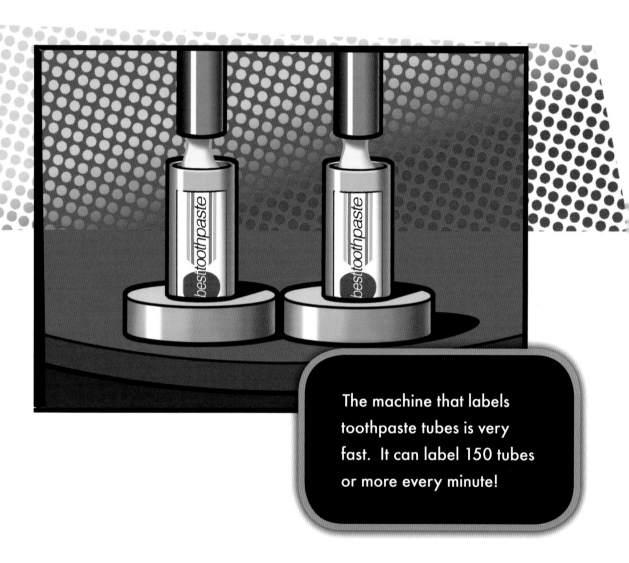

The machine that labels toothpaste tubes is very fast. It can label 150 tubes or more every minute!

A machine fills the tubes with toothpaste.

Many people like toothpaste with stripes. If the toothpaste is white, only one hose fills the toothpaste tubes. To make striped toothpaste, food coloring is added to white toothpaste. Then a separate hose is used for each color. The hoses squirt their colors into a toothpaste tube at the same time. The stripes go from the cap to the end of the tube. Each time you brush, you will have striped toothpaste!

Some toothpaste has stripes.

The tubes continue on the conveyor belt to the sealing machine. This machine pulls the ends of the tubes together. It folds them over and seals them. Finally the tubes are stamped with the date the toothpaste **expires**. Toothpaste can go bad after a certain time.

A date tells you when the toothpaste goes bad.

It will not clean your teeth as well as it should.

Next a machine paints the outside of the tube. It also adds labels to the tubes. A label tells important information about the toothpaste. The label includes the name of the toothpaste and the name of the company that made it. It also shows information about what the toothpaste was made to do. Some toothpaste is made to whiten teeth. Some helps stop **cavities** from forming. Many kinds of toothpaste do many jobs at the same time.

Most kinds of toothpaste prevent cavities.

CHAPTER SIX

Tested and Boxed

The conveyor belt next takes the tubes to an inspector. This worker looks at each tube and pulls out any that are not perfect. Sometimes the label may not have gone on the right way. Or the tube may have a hole in it. A machine weighs the tubes. The weight shows if the right amount of toothpaste is inside. Tubes that are not perfect are not thrown away. Many times they are sold to companies that sell seconds. Seconds are items that have something wrong with them. The box might not

Sometimes labels are not put on right.

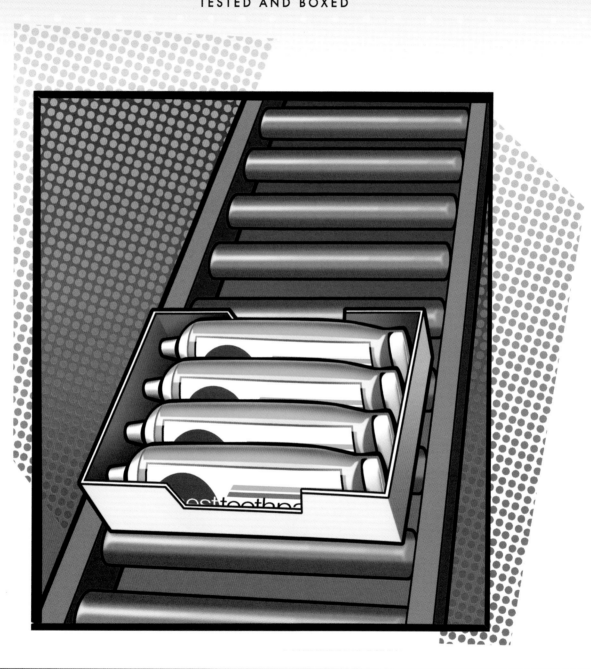

Tubes are boxed and sent to stores.

be perfect or the color may be wrong. People who buy seconds pay much less for the items.

The tubes that pass inspection are boxed. Some companies do this packing by hand. Others do it with machines. The boxes are weighed to make sure each box has the right number of tubes in it. Then the boxes are sealed and stored in the factory's warehouse. The toothpaste is now ready to be shipped to the store.

CHAPTER SEVEN

Onto Your Brush

Toothpaste ships by trucks to neighborhood stores. The new toothpaste tubes might go to a grocery store, a drug store, or a department store. Toothpaste can even be sold at gas stations.

You have lots of choices when you shop for toothpaste. What yummy flavor do you want? Do you want stripes? What do you want your toothpaste to do? Do you want your teeth whiter? Do you want them stronger? Pick a toothpaste you like. And remember to

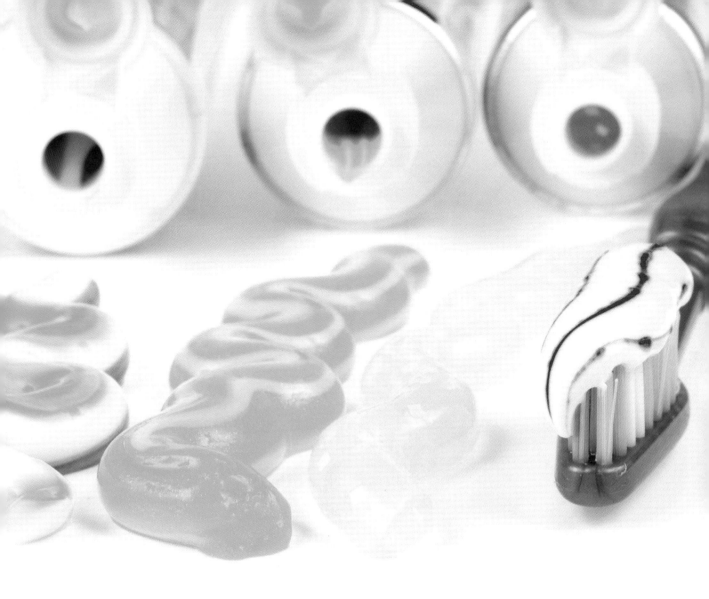

brush your teeth every day. You will have a mouthful of happy, healthy teeth!

TOOTHPASTE MAP

1
INGREDIENTS MIXED

2
BATCH IS COOLED

3
TUBES FILLED

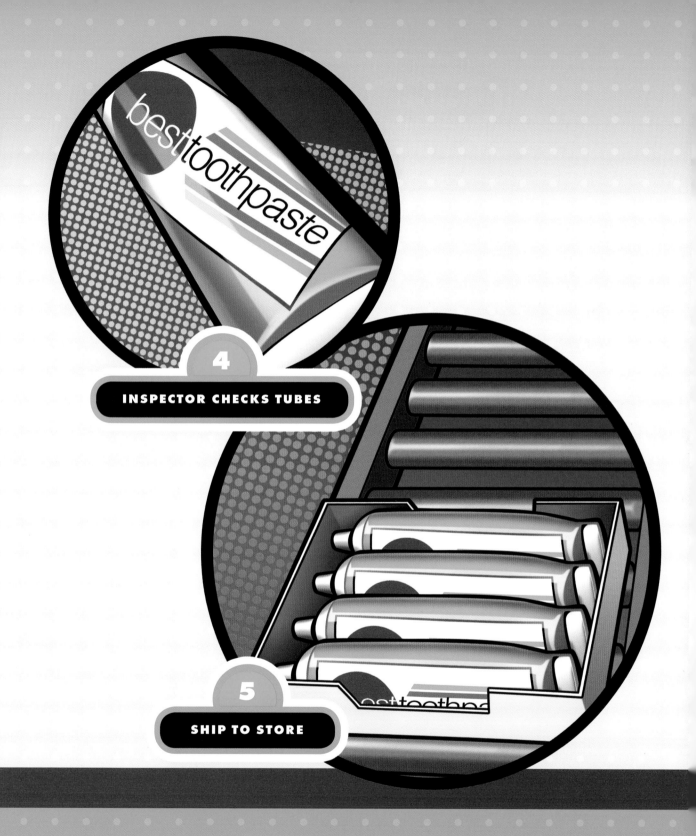

4

INSPECTOR CHECKS TUBES

5

SHIP TO STORE

GLOSSARY

abrasives (uh-BRAY-sivz): Abrasives are materials that are rough and can be used to grind something else. Abrasives help toothpaste remove food from teeth.

cavities (KAV-uh-teez): Cavities are holes in teeth. Using toothpaste helps stop cavities from forming on teeth.

chemicals (KEM-uh-kuhlz): Chemicals are substances made using chemistry. Different chemicals are used in toothpaste.

conveyor belt (kuhn-VAY-ur BELT): A conveyor belt is a moving belt that takes materials from one place to another in a factory. Tubes move on a conveyor belt in the factory.

enamel (i-NAM-uhl): Enamel is the hard, white surface of teeth. Toothpaste helps enamel stay strong.

expires (ek-SPIREZ): Something expires when it reaches the end of the time it can be used. You should not use toothpaste after it expires.

humectant (hyoo-MEK-tant): Humectant is a material that keeps moisture in something. Humectant is a toothpaste ingredient.

ingredients (in-GREE-dee-uhnts): Ingredients are things that are added to a mixture, like items in a recipe list. Different ingredients are used in a toothpaste recipe.

plaque (PLAK): Plaque is a film of bacteria, food, and saliva that is found on the surface of a tooth and can hurt teeth. Toothpaste helps prevent plaque.

preservatives (pri-ZUR-vuh-tivz): Preservatives are chemicals added to foods and drinks to keep them from spoiling. Preservatives make toothpaste last longer.

BOOKS

Curry, Don L. *Take Care of your Teeth*. New York: Scholastic, 2005.

Miller, Edward. *The Tooth Book: A Guide to Healthy Teeth and Gums*. New York: Holiday House, 2009.

Stone, Tanya Lee. *Toothpaste from Start to Finish*. Woodbridge, CT: Blackbirch Press 2001.

INDEX

Visit our Web site for links about toothpaste production: childsworld.com/links

Note to Parents, Teachers, and Librarians: We routinely verify our Web links to make sure they are safe and active sites. So encourage your readers to check them out!